The world's best mom is:

....

Signed:

To my mum, with love, T.K.
For Mum and Dad, and everything you do, J.L.

tiger tales
5 River Road, Suite 128, Wilton, CT 06897
Published in the United States 2014
Originally published in Great Britain 2013
by Hodder Children's Books
a division of Hachette Children's Books
Text copyright © 2013 Timothy Knapman
Illustrations copyright © 2013 Jamie Littler
ISBN-13: 978-1-58925-157-1
ISBN-10: 1-58925-157-1
Printed in China
WKT 0612

For more insight and activities, visit us at www.tigertalesbooks.com

Mom's the Word

by TIMOTHY KNAPMAN

Illustrated by JAMIE LITTLER

tiger tales

What's the word that feels like a **cuddle**? Like splashing and sploshing through a great big **puddle**?

A word like a **party**

when your friends all come?

I can't think;

my head's gone numb!

It's a word as warm as a **good-night kiss.**

There's no other word
that's as good as this.

It's a word like a book at the
end of a fun day.

It's a word that
tastes like an

ice-cream
sundae.

It's a word that **takes** your cares away.

A word like the **park**

where you love to play.

Like the **perfect present** on Christmas Day.

Oh, what's the word
I'm trying to say?

It lifts you up like a
great balloon.

And when you're sick, it means,
"Get well soon!"

It's a word that says,
"I love you so,"

And "Let's have fun!
Away we go!"

It's a word like the
dearest wish you make

When you're blowing
out the candles on your
birthday cake!

It's a word
like the **sun;**
it's warm and bright.
Like a **firework,**
it lights up the
night.

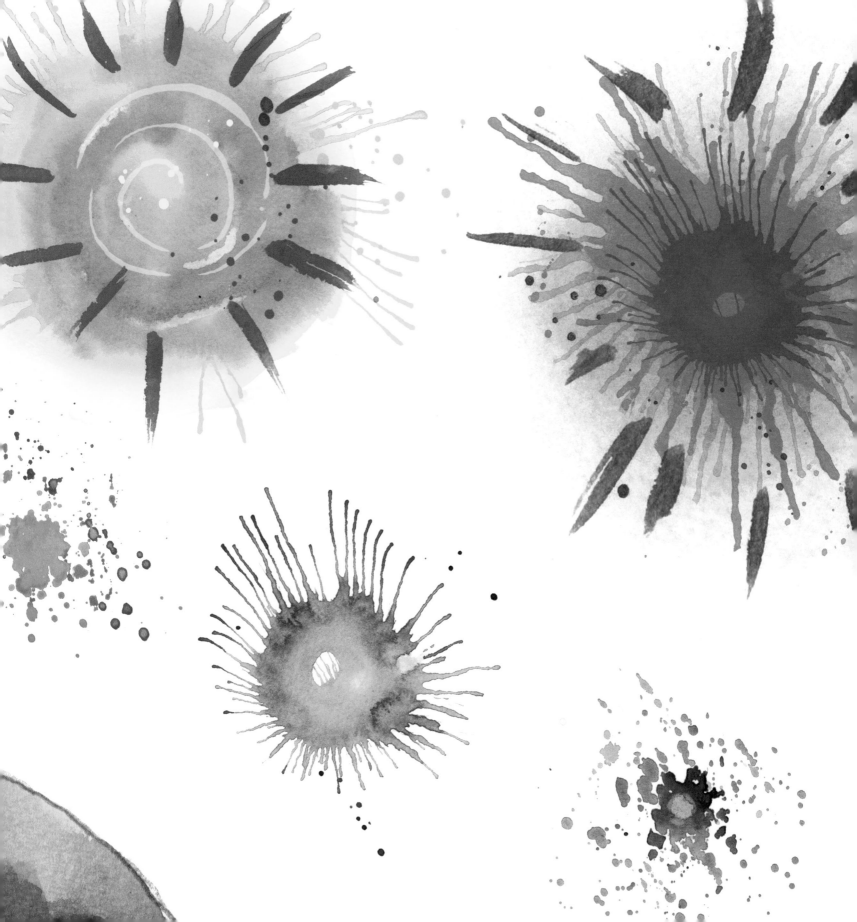

And when you're out in
the dark and rain

And you just can't wait
to get **home** again;

When your own front
door will open wide,

It's the word that keeps
you **warm** inside.

It's a word like a

song you sing along to,

That cheers you up

when you're feeling blue.

It's a word that so much

joy comes from . . . .

I know the word! The word is . . .

"Mom!"